IWA NO KUNI:
THE LAND
OF STONES

SUNA NO KUNI:
THE LAND
OF SAND

THE
FIVE
LANDS

THE FIRE SHADOW

KONOHA NO KUNI
KONOHARGURE
NO SATO:

VILLAGE HIDDEN
IN THE LEAVES

THE WATER SHADOW

KIRO NO KUNI
KIRIGAKURE
NO SATO:

VILLAGE HIDDEN
IN THE MIST

KUMO NO KUNI:
THE LAND OF
THE CLOUDS

KIRO NO KUNI:
THE LAND OF
MIST AND FOG

KONOHA NO KUNI:
THE LAND OF
TREE AND LEAF

THE LIGHTNING SHADOW

KUMO NO KUNI
KUMOGAKURE
NO SATO:

**VILLAGE HIDDEN
IN THE CLOUDS**

THE WIND SHADOW

SUNA NO KUNI
SUNAGAKURE
NO SATO:

**VILLAGE HIDDEN
IN THE SAND**

THE EARTH SHADOW

IWA NO KUNI
IWAGAKURE
NO SATO:

**VILLAGE HIDDEN
IN THE SHADOW**

NARUTO INTRUDERS
CHAPTER BOOK 8

Illustrations: Masashi Kishimoto
Design: Courtney Utt

NARUTO © 1999 by Masashi Kishimoto. All rights reserved.
Original manga first published in Japan in 1999 by SHUEISHA Inc., Tokyo.
This English language chapter book novelization is based on the original manga.
The stories, characters and incidents mentioned in this publication are entirely fictional.

Published by VIZ Media, LLC
P.O. Box 77010
San Francisco, CA 94107

www.viz.com

West, Tracey, 1965-
Intruders / original story by Masashi Kishimoto ; adapted by Tracey West ; [illustrations, Masashi Kishimoto].
  p. cm. -- (Naruto)
"A VIZ Kids Book."
Summary: After many adventures, the time has come for Naruto, Sakura, and Sasuke
to face their most difficult challenge yet--the chunin examination that will determine
whether they are ready to become journeymen, the next level of ninja.
ISBN 978-1-4215-2318-7
[1. Ninja--Fiction. 2. Examinations--Fiction. 3. Schools--Fiction. 4. Japan-
-Fiction.] I. Kishimoto, Masashi, 1974- II. Title.
PZ7.W51937Imt 2009
[Fic]--dc22
                 2008049886

Printed in the U.S.A.
First printing, July 2009

INTRUDERS

ORIGINAL STORY BY **MASASHI KISHIMOTO**

ADAPTED BY TRACEY WEST

vizkids

VIZ MEDIA
SAN FRANCISCO

THE STORY SO FAR

All the ninja in Leaf Village start their training at the Ninja Academy. When they graduate, they qualify to become *genin*—junior ninja.

The genin are put into squads of three with a senior ninja leader—a *jonin*. The squads are paid to perform missions. After several missions, the genin can test to become *chunin*—journeymen ninja.

Naruto, Sasuke, and Sakura belong to Squad Seven, led by a powerful ninja named Kakashi. They have just returned from the Land of Waves, where they helped to save an island from a rogue ninja and an evil gangster. Now they're back in Leaf Village, and their missions are not as exciting.

But things are about to get a lot more interesting…

Naruto
ナルト

Naruto is training to be a ninja. He's a bit of a clown. But deep down, he's serious about becoming the world's greatest shinobi!

Sakura
春野サクラ

Naruto and Sasuke's classmate. She has a crush on Sasuke, who ignores her. In return, she picks on Naruto, who has a crush on *her*.

Sasuke
うちはサスケ

The top student in Naruto's class and a member of the prestigious Uchiha clan.

SUNLIGHT STREAMED through the window of Naruto's room. He sat up, yawned, and stretched. A sleep cap with the eyes and round nose of a penguin sat on top of his head.

Naruto did not feel like waking up. But Kakashi, the leader of Squad Seven, wanted the squad to report for an early morning mission. Naruto yawned again and took off his hat. His yellow hair stuck out all over his head in spikes.

He shuffled across the messy floor like a

zombie. He took a carton of milk from the refrigerator. Then he sat down at the rickety wood table in the center of the room. He still had not cleaned up what was left of last night's dinner. He pushed aside a dirty bowl and an empty noodle packet. Then he poured the milk into a cup.

Naruto drank the milk and ate some slightly stale bread. Then he dressed in his ninja gear: black sandals, orange pants, and an orange and blue jacket. He slipped his ninja tools inside his pockets. First was a small throwing knife called a *kunai*. Then he added some *shuriken*—metal throwing stars.

The last thing Naruto did was tie his dark blue Leaf Village headband around his head. Then he grinned. He felt wide awake now.

Naruto stepped outside into the bright morning light. He raced down the streets of Leaf Village.

"Woo hoo!" Naruto cheered. "No matter what today's mission is, I'll have the energy to face it now!"

He ran even faster. "Start your engines! Mach 5!"

Up ahead, Naruto spotted the other members of his squad. They waited on a wooden bridge, the meeting place Kakashi had chosen. Sakura wore a short red dress over black leggings. Her pale pink hair was the color of cherry blossoms. Sasuke had black hair and wore a dark blue shirt, white pants, and matching wrist guards. Each of them wore a leaf headband just like Naruto's.

"Good morning, *Sakuraaaa!*" Naruto called out.

Naruto ignored Sasuke on purpose. When he got to the bridge, he greeted Sasuke with a glare. Sakura noticed. A dark look crossed her pretty face.

Not again! she silently fumed. *Ever since we got home from the Land of Waves, these two have*

been acting weird! It's sooo embarrassing.

Knock it off, freaks! Sakura's inner voice screamed. Sometimes when she was really angry, or just needed that extra boost of strength, Sakura's inner voice was so loud it almost had a mind of its own. She called the

voice Inner Sakura!

The three ninja waited in silence for Kakashi. They waited...and waited...and waited some more.

Three hours later, Kakashi arrived on the bridge. Their leader wore black pants and a green vest. A black mask covered the bottom half of his face. His leaf headband was pushed over his left eye.

"Good morning, everyone," he said cheer-fully. "I'm afraid I got lost on the way here."

Sakura frowned. "*YOUR NOSE IS GROWING, MASTER!*" she accused.

"Yeah. Not much of an excuse," Naruto agreed.

He jumped in front of Kakashi. "Any hot new missions for Squad Seven?" he asked. "We've had nothing but boring stuff to do. We want a challenge! Some action! Something where I can use all my skills!"

Squad Seven had returned to Leaf Village a few weeks ago after an exciting mission. Lately they had been stuck with boring junior-level missions. They spent a lot of time babysitting and finding lost cats.

Sasuke and Sakura both gave Naruto dirty looks. Naruto knew just what they were thinking.

Grrr. Every time we go on a mission, Sasuke ends up showing me up and saving me. But not this time!

Naruto slipped into a daydream. He imagined saving Sasuke from an enemy attack.

"Saving you is such a nuisance, Sasuke!" That's what I'll tell him. He smiled, thinking about how great that would feel.

"Hey, Naruto, wake up!" Kakashi said. "We're headed to our mission."

"Yes, sir!" Naruto said, snapping to attention.

Sakura shook her head. "Just calm down!"

Squad Seven's mission turned out to be the same as usual. It wasn't very exciting. Naruto tried to show off again and ended up getting hurt.

He leaned against Sakura as they walked down the street.

"You would have been fine if you hadn't overdone it," she scolded him.

"You're a real nuisance," Sasuke added.

"That does it, Sasuke!" Naruto yelled.

Sakura tried to hold him back. "If you start anything more, I'll finish it!"

"Hmm," Kakashi said thoughtfully. "Lately your teamwork has not been so great."

"You tell him!" Naruto yelled, shaking his fist. "You're always messing up our team-work, Sasuke!"

"He was talking to you, pinhead," Sasuke said. "If you're so sick of letting me save you, *why don't you get better than me?*"

He turned to face Naruto. His dark eyes blazed angrily.

I hate this, he thought. *There are guys out there who could challenge me. But I'm stuck on nothing missions with this twerp.*

Sakura watched the two boys stare each other down.

These two are on even worse terms than before! she thought.

How were they supposed to work as a team when they couldn't get along?

KAKASHI LOOKED up at a bird flying high in the sky—a sign from the Hokage.

"I'm going home," Sasuke said. He turned and walked away.

Sakura ran up to him.

"Hey Sasuke, wait up!" she called. "I was wondering if…if the two of us could work on our, um, teamwork?"

Sakura blushed. She had a big crush on Sasuke.

"You're as bad as Naruto," Sasuke replied.

"Why waste your time flirting when you should be training? Even *his* skills are better than yours."

Sakura's Inner Sakura was furious. **WORSE THAN NARUTO? NO WAY!**

Outside, she was crushed and sad. She hung her head as Sasuke walked away.

He's right. It doesn't matter what our mission is. They're all the same to me, she thought darkly, *'cause I'm always the weakest. The one with almost no special skills.*

Naruto saw his chance. "Hey, Sakura! Forget Sasuke. You and I can train together."

Kakashi could always smell trouble brewing. He used his ninja skills to quickly vanish.

Confused, Naruto looked around. "Where

did Master Kakashi go? Is he giving us some alone time?"

Sakura didn't answer. She walked away from Naruto, staring at the sidewalk.

"Whatever!" Naruto said. "What matters is I'm done losing. There's only one thing ahead of me, and that's training!" He started to follow Sakura.

Rustle. Rustle.

"Huh?" The strange sound made Naruto turn around.

A box sat on the stone walkway behind him. Somebody had drawn lines on the box to make it look like a rock. Two eyeholes were cut in the end of the box.

Why is a rock sneaking up on me? Naruto wondered.

He casually turned back around. He took a few more steps. Then...

"Psych!" Naruto yelled, spinning around. "Faked you out, rock! No rock has perfect corners and eyeholes. Kind of a big clue."

He heard grunting as the box wobbled back and forth. Then three kids jumped out from under it.

"Tadaaaaaaaaaaaa!"

The cry came from their leader, a boy with spiky black hair and a long scarf around his neck that trailed behind him on the ground. A boy with glasses and a runny nose and a tiny girl with two ponytails stood with him. Each one wore green goggles on their forehead.

"Leave it to the man I have acknowledged as being almost my equal. Your skills rival my own," the leader said.

"Oh, it's you guys," Naruto said, relieved.

The black-haired boy was Konohamaru, the grandson of Lord Hokage. Lord Hokage was the leader of Leaf Village. Konohamaru acted like a great ninja, but he was just a little kid. Naruto had known him for a while and knew that Konohamaru looked up to him a lot. Konohamaru felt like people treated him weirdly because he was the grandson of the Hokage. Naruto knew what it was like to be shunned for being different or strange. So even though Konohamaru was a pain, Naruto tried to be nice to him.

"What's up with the goggles?" Naruto asked.

Konohamaru laughed. "You're our idol, right? They're just like the ones you used to wear."

Naruto used to wear goggles every day— before he got his leaf headband. He wasn't sure how he felt about three goofy kids copying him.

"Okaaaay," he said.

"What do you mean, okay?" Konohamaru yelled. "Suddenly too cool for school, big guy?"

Naruto sighed. "What do you want from me?"

"We'll show you, boss," the little girl answered eagerly. "Can you come now?"

"Nope!" Naruto replied. "I have to train!"

Konohamaru stomped his foot. "But you promised to play ninja with us, right?" he yelled.

"Heh," Naruto said. He knew the boy was right. "Was that today?"

He had to find a way out of it. *If I play with them even a little, they'll waste my whole day!*

Sakura walked over to them. She was still miserable.

KONOHAMARU TURNED to Naruto and asked, "Hey, big guy? Who's the babe?"

Sakura glared at Naruto. She looked mad—but he liked it.

The way she's looking at me...stop! I'm blushing.

Konohamaru tried to figure out what was going on.

That girl's eyeing him like she wants to battle him, he thought. But he didn't know what that meant.

Then it hit him. He punched Naruto in the arm. "Hey big guy, it makes sense, seeing how smart and cool you are and everything," he said. He winked. *SHE'S YOUR GIRLFRIEND, RIGHT?"*

Naruto blushed even more. "You little guys catch on quick!"

"**WRONG!**"

Furious, Sakura punched Naruto. He slammed into the sidewalk and skidded down the street.

"Big guy!" Konohamaru yelled.

He and his friends ran to Naruto's side. Naruto groaned. He had a big bump on top of his head.

"You're our leader! You can't die!" Konohamaru said dramatically.

He looked up at Sakura. "What did you do that for?" he yelled. "Are you a girl or some kind of monster?"

Sakura's eyes went black. She slammed a fist into her palm.

LET ME AT 'EM! her Inner Sakura screamed.

Naruto jumped up. He knew what was coming.

"RUUUUUUUN!" he yelled.

Sakura charged. Naruto and the kids ran down the street.

POW!

Konohamaru slammed into something. He looked up.

Two ninja had appeared out of nowhere. One was a boy in black clothing with purple markings painted on his face. He wore a head-band marked with a strange symbol. There was something bulky strapped to his back. It was wrapped in cloth like a mummy.

A girl ninja stood next to him. She had

her hands on her hips and looked angry. Her sandy-colored hair was tied in four jagged ponytails. Her headband was tied around her neck. She wore a short purple jacket with long sleeves.

"That's gotta smart," the boy ninja said.

4

THE NINJA grabbed the little boy by his scarf. With one hand, he lifted him off the ground.

"Konohamaru!" Naruto cried.

The ninja just smiled. "That hurt, snot-face," he told Konohamaru.

"Knock it off, Kankuro," the girl ninja warned. "You're gonna get it as it is."

"It's my fault," Sakura apologized. "I was fooling around."

Naruto's eyes blazed. *"PUT HIM DOWN!"*

Kankuro didn't
look worried. *These
guys must be* genin
from Leaf Village,
the ninja guessed.
He grinned.

"I just want to play with him a little," he
said in a sinister voice. "We're waiting for
someone."

He tightened his grip on Konohamaru.
The boy cried out.

Naruto had all he could take. He charged
at Kankuro. The ninja motioned for Naruto
to bring it on.

"You rotten—"

SLAM!

Naruto crashed into some kind of invisible

force field. He flew backward and tumbled to the ground.

"What was that?" Naruto asked.

"What a wimp," Kankuro sneered. "Is that the best the genin of the Leaf Village can do?"

Sakura suddenly noticed their headbands.

They're not from around here, she realized. *What do they want?*

Meanwhile, Kakashi was at Ninja Academy delivering his mission report. Other jonin —senior ninja—like Kakashi sat on benches, trading stories about their squads. Four academy teachers, or sensei, sat at a long desk to take the reports.

One of the teachers was Master Iruka. He had taught Squad Seven when they were cadets at the Ninja Academy. He had a kind face and a long scar across his nose. He wore his black hair in a short ponytail.

Master Iruka had a special bond with Naruto. The boy had saved his life once.

The meeting of the jonin was suddenly interrupted by a message from the Hokage. He had sent the bird Kakashi had seen earlier to summon all the senior ninja. All of the squad leaders and teachers were called to meet the Hokage in his hall.

Lord Hokage sat behind an important-looking desk at the end of the hall. The old man wore a hat with long cloth panels that hung down the sides of his face.

"You may be able to guess what we are here to discuss," Lord Hokage began.

"Is it time already?" Kakashi asked.

Another jonin beside him spoke up. "Have you told the leaders of the other lands yet?" he asked. "Because I have already seen some of them in our village. When is it to be?"

"One week from today," Lord Hokage replied.

The squad leaders looked surprised. "Isn't this rather sudden?" someone asked.

"It is final," Lord Hokage said firmly. His tone told the other ninja not to argue. "Seven days from now, on July first, we shall begin the Chunin Selection Exam, the tests that will decide who will become journeymen, the next level of ninja!"

THE LITTLE boy and girl called out for their friend, worried.

"Konohamaru!"

They helped Naruto to his feet. He was angrier than ever now.

"Hey! You in the black pig suit!" he taunted, pointing at Kankuro. "Let go of him now and I'll go easy on you, loser!"

Sakura pulled Naruto back.

"You're the loser!" she yelled. "Do you want that guy to pound you again?"

"You're starting to annoy me," Kankuro sneered. "You better show me some respect, or this kid's gonna get it."

Naruto and Sakura were shocked. What kind of ninja would hurt a little kid? Konohamaru's friends shivered with fright.

The girl ninja turned her back to Kankuro. "I will not be held responsible for this," she said. But she didn't try to stop him.

WHO IS HE? Sakura wondered. *This is* so *not good.*

Kankuro lifted Konohamaru another foot off the ground. "So, I'll finish with this tiny shrimp and then take care of that other jumbo shrimp over there," he said, nodding to Naruto.

"YOU!" Naruto yelled.

"YOU! YOU—" He charged at Kankuro once more.

THOCK!

A rock smacked into Kankuro's wrist and clattered to the ground. The ninja grunted in pain and dropped the little boy.

Sasuke sat calmly in the branch of a tree overlooking them. He tossed two more rocks in his hand.

"It's Sasuke!" Sakura cheered.

Naruto frowned. "So?"

Kankuro glared at Sasuke. The girl ninja with him gazed at Sasuke with a slight smile.

Hmm. He's pretty cool!

Meanwhile, in Lord Hokage's hall, the village leader continued the meeting.

"Now we'd like to hear from the squad leaders who are training our newest junior ninja," he said.

Kakashi stepped forward with two other jonin. Kurenai was a slender woman with wavy black hair and strange red eyes. Asuma was a big man with black hair and a beard.

"Tell us," Lord Hokage said. "Do any of you have genin who are ready to take the chunin exam? They must have completed at least eight missions. Beyond that, it is up to you to decide if they are ready."

Master Iruka stood among the teachers in the group. He frowned.

He shouldn't be asking this yet, he thought. *It's too soon for any of them.*

"You may begin, Kakashi," Lord Hokage said.

"The members of Squad Seven are Sasuke, Naruto, and Sakura," he said. "I vow upon my clan, the Hatake, that all three of them are ready for the chunin exam."

6

"WHAT?" IRUKA cried out.

Kurenai spoke next. "The members of Squad Eight are Hinata, Kiba, and Shino," she said. "I vow upon my own clan, the Yuhi, that all three are ready for the chunin exam. I am as certain as Kakashi."

Asuma spoke in a gruff voice. "The members of Squad Ten are Ino, Shikamaru, and Choji. I vow upon my clan, the Sarutobi, that I am also certain. All three are ready for the chunin exam."

Iruka stepped forward. "Just a moment," he said nervously.

"Yes, Iruka?" Lord Hokage asked.

"Lord Hokage, please allow me to speak," the sensei said. "Forgive me if I overstep my rank, but I taught the nine students just named. They are all gifted, but it's too soon for kids that young to be stepping up to the journeyman level."

Master Iruka grew bolder as he spoke. "They need more experience before they take these exams," he said. "I don't understand why their squad leaders can't see that."

"I was six years younger than Naruto when I became a chunin, Iruka," Kakashi pointed out.

"Naruto's not like you!" Iruka said angrily.

"Do you want to destroy those children?"

"They gripe about every detail of a mission," Kakashi replied. "Just for once, I think it would do them good to find out what real pain is. Let's admit it. Breaking them would be fun."

Iruka was horrified. "Are you out of your mind?"

"It was just a joke, Master Iruka," Kakashi said calmly. "I understand you. And I'm sorry if my decision upsets you. But I stand by it."

Iruka did not back down. "But—"

"Kakashi, can we finish with this?" Kurenai asked.

Kakashi looked Iruka in the eye. "It's none of your business anyway," he said firmly. "They're not your students anymore. **THEY ARE SOLDIERS UNDER MY COMMAND.**"

Iruka gritted his teeth. He hated it, but Kakashi was right.

There was nothing he could do.

Back outside, Konohamaru quickly ran away from Kankuro. The ninja gazed at Sasuke, who was still perched in the tree.

"Oh look. Another little brat," he said.

"Get lost," Sasuke replied.

Sakura and the kids stared at Sasuke like he was a star.

"Oooh, how cool!" Sakura said.

Konohamaru pointed at Naruto. "You stink!"

"I could have beaten that loser if Sasuke didn't butt in!" Naruto protested.

The boy wouldn't even look at him. "Yeah, right."

Naruto was furious again. *He did it again—getting in my way and making me look bad!*

Kankuro had lost interest in Naruto and the others. He called up to Sasuke.

"Come down, little squirrel!"

Sasuke just stared at him.

Kankuro grinned. "You think you're pretty smart, don't you?"

With one quick move, he unfurled the object on his back. Sasuke could see black hair sticking out from the mummy wrapping. Did

Kankuro have some kind of *person* in there?

The girl ninja gasped. "Tell me you're not planning to use the Crow!"

The ninja began to unwrap the strange object.

"KANKURO, DON'T!"

Sasuke froze. The cry came from right next to him. But how could that be?

A boy hung upside down from the next tree branch. His feet stuck to the bottom of the branch. It looked like magic, but Sasuke knew the boy used powerful chakra to hang like that.

"Kankuro, **YOU'RE A DISGRACE** to our entire village," the boy said coldly.

NARUTO AND the others stared at the new-comer. The boy had reddish-brown hair. His green eyes were ringed with thick black lines. He had a mark above his left eye that looked like a tattoo.

"G-Gaara," Kankuro said. He flashed a nervous smile. Even though Gaara was younger, Kankuro looked like a little boy caught doing something bad.

He snuck up on me, Sasuke thought. *I didn't have a clue! His skill rivals Kakashi's.*

"It annoys me that you'd lose control in a quarrel with children," Gaara told Kankuro. "Have you forgotten why we came here?"

"But Gaara, they started it!" Kankuro whined. "The little one slammed into me!"

"Shut up," Gaara said. *"Or I'll destroy you."*

Kankuro shivered. "You're right," he said quickly. "I was out of line. We're sorry, okay? Really, really sorry." Gaara turned his head to look at Sasuke. "Sorry about my friends."

Sasuke studied him. *So he's in charge, eh? He has eyes like a snake.*

Suddenly, Gaara began to spin. His body seemed to transform into grains of swirling sand. He floated down to the ground. He

G-GAA-RA...

kept his eyes on Sasuke the whole time.

He nailed Kankuro with a stone. That took skill, thought Gaara.

Gaara landed between Kankuro and the girl ninja. Sasuke could see that Gaara carried a huge jug on his back.

"I know we're a little early, but we didn't come here to play around," he said.

"I swear it won't happen again!" Kankuro promised.

Gaara began to walk down the street. "Kankuro, Temari, let's go."

"Wait!" Sakura called out. She ran after them.

"Yes?" Gaara asked.

"Your headbands show that you're from the Village Hidden in the Sand," Sakura said. "Your country is one of our allies. But your ninja are not permitted here without authorization."

Her ninja training kicked in. She had to protect Leaf Village—no matter how tough these intruders seemed.

"State your business!" she demanded. "We can't just let you go your merry way."

Temari held up a travel pass. "Didn't you know?" she asked. "As you guessed, we're junior-level ninja from the Village Hidden in the Sand. We're here to take the chunin exam."

"What's the chunin exam?" Naruto asked.

"You really don't know?" Temari asked. She shook her head. "Junior ninja from other lands are sent here to compete against the Leaf Village candidates."

"Why test all of us together?" Naruto asked.

"Mainly, it's to make sure the ninja are all on the same skill level," she replied. "Also to foster friendship and understanding between ninja. And of course—"

Naruto turned to Konohamaru. "Hey, maybe I should enter this chunin exam thing, huh? Right?"

Temari shook her fist at him. "Listen! When you ask someone a question, it's good manners to listen to their entire answer."

Sasuke jumped down from the tree and faced the three ninja.

"Hey, you there! What's your name?"

Temari blushed. "Who? Me?"

"No!" Sasuke replied. "The creepy guy next to you."

Temari and Kankuro looked shocked to hear somebody speak to Gaara like that.

"**GAARA OF THE DESERT**, at your service," Gaara replied. "And you are…?"

"Sasuke Uchiha."

The two boys stared at each other for a moment.

"Hey! Hey!" Naruto called out. "Don't you want to know my name?"

"No," Gaara said simply. He turned and walked away.

THE THREE ninja from the Sand Village quickly disappeared.

Sasuke watched them go, grinning slightly.

Things are getting interesting, he thought.

Naruto sat down, dejected. "Konohamaru, am I really such a loser?" he asked.

The boy nodded. "Next to Sasuke, you are, big guy."

"Sasuke!" Naruto yelled. "You have to stop sticking your nose in my business! I am not gonna take this!"

Sasuke was right. Things were getting very interesting in Leaf Village. Squads of ninja from different villages were starting to arrive.

One squad watched the scene between Squad Seven and the ninja from the Sand Village. They stayed hidden on the branch of a nearby tree.

All three wore camouflage pants. Each one covered the bottom half of their face with a scarf.

"What do you think?" one of the masked ninja asked.

"None of them are of any importance," replied their leader. "Except the raven-hair from Leaf Village and the creep from the

Sand. Keep an eye on them."

And in the nearby woods, another squad from Leaf Village was training. Tenten, a pretty young girl with black hair, was throwing kunai into a straw figure. The human-shaped target was attached to a tree. Bull's-eyes were painted on the straw figure's body.

Neji, a boy with long, straight black hair, watched her practice. He calmly sat at the base of the tree, right underneath the target.

Another boy wearing a dark green bodysuit ran up to them. His shiny black hair was cut in a bowl-shape around his head. He had dark eyes and very thick black eyebrows.

"Hey! Hey! Did you hear?" the boy in the green suit asked. His name was Rock Lee. "The chunin exam is coming up. Word is they're letting members of the rookie class compete for the first time in five years!"

"No way!" Tenten exclaimed. She twirled a kunai as she talked. "It probably has something to do with the jonin elite. I've heard they like to compete with each other."

"I doubt that," Rock Lee answered. "They say three of them are in a squad trained by Kakashi."

"*The* Kakashi? That's interesting," Neji remarked.

Tenten eyed the target. "Well, either way—" she began.

THUNK! THUNK! THUNK!

The weapons all made their mark—in the target just inches above Neji's head.

"It all has a very sad sound to it," he finished.

THE NEXT morning, Squad Seven met on the bridge again. Sakura was still feeling down.

As usual, they waited for Kakashi. And waited…and waited…

Sakura stomped back and forth across the bridge. "Okay, look! Are we just going to stand around and let him get away with this? Why is it, whenever we get called out, we end up waiting around?"

Naruto pumped his fist in the air. "She's right!" he cheered. "Say it, Sakura!"

"I mean, think how I feel!" Sakura fumed. "I overslept. And I didn't even get to blow-dry my hair!"

"Yeah, it's not right!" Naruto agreed. "I overslept too. And I didn't even get to wash my face or brush my teeth!"

Sakura made a face. "**Ew! Gross!**"

Why are these two always so hyper? Sasuke wondered.

Suddenly, Kakashi appeared on top of one

of the bridge's rails.

"Good morning, guys!" he called down. "I guess I got a bit lost on the path of life this morning."

"You are such a liar!" Naruto and Sakura yelled together.

"In any case." Kakashi jumped down. "This may surprise you, but I've recommended all three of you for the Chunin Selection Exam."

"*SAY WHAT?*" Sakura cried.

"Good one, Master," Naruto said. "You almost had us."

Kakashi held out three pieces of paper. "You have to fill out applications."

Naruto couldn't believe it. Kakashi was telling the truth! He jumped on Kakashi, throwing his arms around his neck.

"Master Kakashi! *I LOVE YOU!*"

"Get off!" Kakashi cried. "You're embarrassing me!"

Naruto backed off and took his application.

"If any of you don't wish to take the exam, you don't have to," Kakashi explained. "The choice is yours. If you want to apply, report to room 301 at the school tomorrow afternoon."

Kakashi nodded. "That's all," he said. Then he vanished.

The three ninja walked across the bridge. Naruto was cheerful. Sakura was still miserable. And Sasuke was deep in thought, as always.

Naruto hummed happily as he walked. "Dum di dum. The chunin exam!"

"I bet there will be a lot of tough competition," Sakura said glumly.

Yeah, Naruto agreed silently. *Like that bully with the mummy thing on his back.*

He glanced at Sasuke. *And that show-off over there. I swear, I'm not gonna let anyone beat me!*

Naruto imagined stomping the competition. In his mind, he held a giant trophy cup over his head while Sasuke sulked at his feet.

If I could win something this big, I could be the next Lord Hokage! Naruto daydreamed. He pictured the old man sitting sadly in a corner.

I'LL BET THERE'LL BE A LOT OF TOUGH COMPETITION.

TAK

DUM-DI-DI-DUH... THE JOURNEYMAN NINJA SELECTION EXAM!

TAK

"Replaced by Naruto. I guess the best man won!" the Hokage would say. *"Time for this old man to retire!"*

Then Naruto would get to wear Lord Hokage's hat. Everyone in the village would look up to him. He laughed just thinking about it.

Sasuke was lost in his own daydream. Gaara had shown great skill yesterday.

I might get to face off against that creep, Sasuke hoped. He shivered with anticipation.

It was just the challenge he craved.

The only one not dreaming of the challenge was Sakura. She stopped and let the boys walk ahead of her.

Forget Sasuke, she thought. *I can't even keep up with Naruto. How will I ever pass the chunin exam?*

THE NEXT day, Naruto, Sasuke, and Sakura met at room 301 of Ninja Academy. The hallway in front of the room was crowded with ninja hoping to apply.

The door was guarded by two scruffy-looking young ninja. Rock Lee sat on the floor in front of them. His face was bruised.

"What a loser!" the first guard said. "Are you really going to apply?"

Tenten stepped forward. "Please. We're begging you. Let us in."

Rock Lee got to his feet. He rushed at the guards.

THUD!

The red-nosed guard snorted. "We're saving a step by weeding out the obvious losers now."

Sasuke stepped to the front of the group. "You'd better let me through," he said calmly. "And drop the force-field illusion while you're at it. I need to get to the *THIRD FLOOR.*"

"We're on the third floor," said a confused genin.

The guards laughed.

"So you figured that out, eh?" said the first one.

"It was easy, right Sakura?" Sasuke asked, turning to his teammate. "You were probably the first to notice it."

Sakura wasn't sure what Sasuke was getting at. Then he winked at her.

"You're the best in our squad at understanding the art of illusion," he said.

Sakura suddenly realized that Sasuke was giving her a chance to shine. She wasn't going to let him down.

"Of course I noticed it," she said confidently. "Obviously, we're still on the second floor."

The illusion faded. The sign on the door reading "301" now read "201." The two ninja had tricked them!

"Hey, not bad," said the red-nosed guard. "But just seeing through it isn't... ENOUGH!"

He moved quickly to attack Sasuke. Sasuke countered with a kick. But someone moved faster than both of them.

Rock Lee jumped between them with lightning speed. He grabbed the guard's leg in one hand and Sasuke's leg in the other.

He's so fast! Sakura thought. *He saw the planned attack on both sides and planted himself between their kicks. Is that even possible?*

Rock Lee released both ninja. Sasuke

landed firmly on his feet. The guard toppled to the floor.

He blocked my kick! Sasuke realized.

Rock Lee hopped back to his friends. Then he spotted Sakura and stopped.

"Hi, my name is Rock Lee," he said, blushing. "You're Sakura, right?"

Sakura nodded.

Rock Lee winked. "Would you like to go out with me?" He gave her a thumbs-up. "I'll protect you with my life!"

Sakura was too stunned to answer for a moment.

"No. Way," she said finally. "You are way out of line!"

This exam is turning into a freak show! Sasuke thought.

But Sakura's sad mood was gone. She had seen through the illusion! Maybe she had what it took to be a chunin after all.

"Sasuke, Naruto, let's go!" she cried.

The three friends raced down the hall. They had to get to the third floor.

The chunin exam was set to begin. And Squad Seven was ready!

Ninja Terms

Nindo
A shinobi's *ninja way*, a moral code a ninja follows to stay on the path of good.

Jutsu
Jutsu means "arts" or "techniques." Sometimes referred to as *ninjutsu*, which means more specifically the jutsu of a ninja.

Bunshin
Translated as "doppelganger," this is the art of creating multiple versions of yourself.

Sensei
Teacher

Shuriken
A ninja weapon,
a throwing star

Chunin Selection Exam
The test that determines which young ninja become journeymen.

About the Authors

Author/artist **Masashi Kishimoto** was born in 1974 in rural Okayama Prefecture, Japan. After spending time in art college, he won the Hop Step Award for new manga artists with his manga *Karakuri* (Mechanism). Kishimoto decided to base his next story on traditional Japanese culture. His first version of *Naruto*, drawn in 1997, was a one-shot story about fox spirits; his final version, which debuted in *Weekly Shonen Jump* in 1999, quickly became the most popular ninja manga in Japan. This book is based on that manga.

. . . . . .

Tracey West is the author of more than 150 books for children and young adults, including the *Pixie Tricks* and *Scream Shop* series. An avid fan of cartoons, comic books, and manga, she has appeared on the New York Times Best Seller List as the author of the Pokémon chapter book adaptations. She currently lives with her family in New York State's Hudson Valley.

The Story of Naruto continues in:
Chapter Book 9
The Challengers

Rock Lee is obnoxious, rude, and he really rubs Sakura the wrong way! But he's only one of the challengers that Naruto and his friends meet when it comes time for their new exams. Can Naruto, Sakura, and Sasuke set aside their differences in time to team up against all the other ninja?

#1 THE BOY NINJA
#2 THE TESTS OF A NINJA
#3 THE WORST JOB
#4 THE SECRET PLAN
#5 BRIDGE OF COURAGE
#6 SPEED
#7 THE NEXT LEVEL
#8 INTRUDERS

COMING SOON!
#9 THE CHALLENGERS